GALAXY PATROL

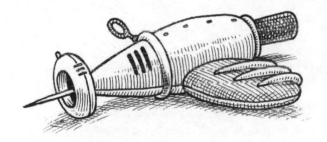

Jean Ure
Illustrated by Mark Oliver

A & C Black • London

First published 2010 by
A & C Black Publishers Ltd
36 Soho Square, London, W1D 3QY

www.acblack.com

ISBN: 978-1-4081-1155-0

A CIP catalogue for this book is available from the British Library.

This book is produced using paper that is made from wood grown in
managed, sustainable forests. It is natural, renewable and recyclable.
The logging and manufacturing processes conform to the
environmental regulations of the country of origin.

Printed and bound in Great Britain
by CPI Cox & Wyman, Reading RG1 8EX.

Chapter One

Last summer, I was abducted by aliens. One minute I was sitting there, in front of the television: the next minute, I'd vanished. I mean it! Completely vanished. My brain was still whizzing about, but the rest of me had gone.

The question was, gone where? I felt like I'd been scrambled. Scattered, in a million pieces. But I could see bits of what looked like body – *my* body – floating past me. A finger, a toe. A nose. *My* nose! My *knee*. The one with the scar, where I'd come off my bike. My arm, still in its green sweater. An *eyeball*. What was going on here?

And then it hit me... I was caught in a transporter beam!

I'd been watching one of Dad's old *Star Treks* when it happened. Captain Kirk had just told Scotty to beam him up – when *I* got beamed up.

My sister had been there, supposedly doing her homework. She wasn't meant to be there, she was meant to be up in her room. As Mum always says, 'How can you concentrate when the television is turned on?' The truth is, she can't. *I* can, 'cos I have extra powers of concentration. If I was doing my homework and the television was on, I would simply blot it out. Rosie, on the other hand, has no powers of concentration. I sometimes think her mind is full of ping-pong balls, all bobbing up and down. And, unlike the television, her voice is practically *impossible* to blot out.

Every few seconds it was, 'I don't know how you can watch this stuff. Honestly, it's so stupid! Little green men? *Death* rays? Oh, please!' And then she would go, 'You! Jake!' and prod me in the ribs with one of her bony fingers. 'You listening? I said it's stupid! Stupid *boy* stuff.'

She can pack a whole load of scorn into her voice, can Rosie. Just because she'd rather watch stupid *girl* stuff. All pink and shrieky. I pointed out that so far not a single little green man had appeared, but she just did this impatient clicking thing with her tongue and said, 'Aliens, then! It's all the same. They don't have to be green … it's still stupid.'

'For all you know,' I told her, 'aliens could be all around us.'

'Oh, yeah?' She made a scoffing sound. 'Haven't seen much evidence of it.'

'There,' I said. I pointed. 'On the screen… What's that? You don't think they just pluck these things out of nowhere?'

She looked at me, like, *un-be-lievable*.

'It's a *story*,' she said. 'It's *made up*. Dumbo!'

I was prepared to agree that the actual storyline was made up. 'But all the other stuff,' I said. 'Spaceships, for instance. Spaceships exist!'

She looked at me again. This time it was more like, *pathetic*.

'Well, they do,' I said. I know about these things; I've done research. 'Those people that have seen flying saucers ... they can't *all* be imagining it. And warp drive! Bending space. Everyone knows *that's* possible – well, in theory. We just haven't quite got there yet. But that's not to say that other life forms haven't!'

'Yeah yeah yeah,' said Rosie, going back to her laptop. 'Just button it, I've got homework to do.'

She clicked furiously for a bit, giving me a few minutes peace and quiet; but, like I say, she has no powers of concentration. I don't think girls do. Not most of them. That's why they can manage about a hundred things all at once. My powers of concentration are so great that I can only do one thing at a time. And right then I was trying to watch *Star Trek*. Dad has boxes and boxes of the DVDs. I know them all practically by heart, but it is still very irritating to be constantly interrupted by ignorant remarks. Or, in this case, a sudden shriek of laughter.

'What is *that* supposed to be?'

I gritted my teeth. 'That,' I said, 'is a creature from another planet. Otherwise known as an extraterrestrial.'

'You mean, an alien.'

'Well, yes. Except…' I frowned. 'I'm not really sure we ought to call them that.'

'You just did! Just now!'

I said, 'Yes, I know, but it's not politically correct. They're just different life forms, that's all.'

'Huh!' She tossed her head. 'Some life form. Looks like a perambulating octopus.'

I nearly said 'You what?' but thought better of it. She's always trying to confuse me by using words I've never heard of.

'Actually,' I said. 'It could be deadly.'

'So what's he going to do? Your hero – Captain *Kirk*. What's he going to do? Get it with his ray gun? Psht!' She made her fingers into a gun shape and aimed them at the screen. 'Zap! And then it explodes, blood and guts all over the place… I s'pose the blood's some yucky colour, like yellow, or something.'

'This particular extraterrestrial,' I informed her, 'doesn't happen to have any blood. It doesn't have blood of *any* colour. And Captain Kirk,' I added, 'does not have a ray gun. Ray guns,' I said, 'are simply figments of your imagination.'

'Oh.' She sniggered. 'Pardon me! So what's all this stuff? I thought it was science *fiction*.'

It is science fiction based on fact. That is what she cannot grasp. She likes to pretend it's all just nonsense. She was about to learn...

'Oops!' She fluttered her hands, pretending to be scared. 'Watch out! It's got him in its tentacles. Now what's going to happen?'

I said, 'He'll tell Scotty to beam him up.'

'Yay! The famous transporter! Wish they'd hurry up and invent it. I could do with one of them for getting me out of maths lessons.'

Rosie is dumb at maths. She seems to think it's amusing, having to add up on her fingers. She does know a lot of long words, though; I'll give her that. But I reckon maths is more important, 'specially if you want to understand temporal mechanics. Ha! She wouldn't even know what that was.

'Matter of fact,' I said, carelessly, 'they already have transporters.'

Her lip curled. 'Who does?'

She never believes a thing I tell her.

I said I wasn't sure exactly *who*. 'It might still just be alien technology. But they do exist.'

She opened her mouth to say 'Oh, yeah?' She is always saying 'Oh, yeah?' Anything she can't argue against. *Oh, yeah*? Only this time she didn't get the chance, 'cos at that very moment Captain Kirk spoke into his communicator: 'Beam me up, Scotty!' And that was when I disappeared...

Chapter Two

Whoosh! I'd landed.

Some of me had landed. I could feel that some bits were still missing. The odd toe. The nose. My right ear.

Well, that was OK; I wasn't too anxious about it. I knew that body parts didn't always reassemble themselves at exactly the same moment. Some of them were probably still floating around in the transporter. Yup! That was my nose. Back in the middle of my face, right where it ought to be. Oh, and here came the toes! A whole bunch of them. I hadn't realised so many were missing. Now I was just waiting for my right ear.

'Ere, 'ere. Dad would make a joke of that. Dad makes jokes about everything. But I bet even he wouldn't make a joke if he were all exploded into atoms and having to wait while he got put together again. It might have been a bit scary if I hadn't seen it so often on *Star Trek*. Of course,

there was the occasional accident, when people *didn't* get put back together ... but most of me was back. I guess you can live without a right ear.

BOY LOSES EAR IN TRANSPORTER ACCIDENT. I could already see the headline in the local paper. Not that anyone would believe it, 'cos people never do. They wouldn't have to, anyway, 'cos suddenly there it was. Back! A big flapping elephant's ear stuck to the side of my head. (It's Rosie who says I have elephant's ears. She can talk! She has a nose like a *blob*.)

Now that I was all in one piece, I could concentrate on my surroundings. Where had I been brought? A spaceship, that was for sure. I could recognise the inside of a spaceship when I saw one. Seemed like they'd beamed me direct to the control deck. Wow! Serious stuff. Whoever they were, they obviously meant business.

Some of them were standing there, watching, as my body reassembled itself. Two men and a woman. They all wore uniforms, like black tracksuits with coloured logos. They didn't *look* like aliens... I mean different life forms. Creatures from other planets. But they obviously had to be.

Humans might have gone to the moon, and Mars, and places like that, but we hadn't yet invented transporters. Not as far as I was aware. Only other life forms had those. We *knew* about them; but we didn't actually have them. Which meant that these three people weren't really people at all...

They were *pretending* to be people. It was obviously some kind of disguise. Some kind of cloak they wrapped themselves in to fool you. Or to make you feel more comfortable, depending on what sort of life forms they were. Friendly, or ... the other sort. It wasn't really possible to tell.

One of the men stepped forward. He had a red logo with gold stripes, so I guessed he had to be the captain. The others only had silver, and only one stripe each. The captain had three. He raised a hand, very solemnly, palm upward. I raised mine back; it seemed only polite. Unless it was some kind of threat? No! He was smiling. A friendly smile, like Captain Kirk. Now his lips were moving. What was he saying? I couldn't hear anything. There wasn't any sound! Had I gone deaf? I rubbed at my right ear, checking that it really had come back.

'I beg your pardon.' The captain pressed a little button in the middle of his logo and his voice came booming out. 'A translator blip. Forgive me. I say again… Hail, Earthlings!'

Earthlings? How many of us were there? Don't say my body had reassembled itself into two!

And then, from somewhere behind me, a familiar voice spoke. It sounded a bit irritable.

'Well, hail to *you*,' it said, 'but d'you mind telling us what's going on?'

Rosie! What was *she* doing here? What could anyone possibly want with her? And why did she have to be so rude?

'I mean, for starters,' she said, 'where exactly are we?'

Such bad manners. We were guests in this spaceship! If I'd been the captain, I'd have told her to watch herself. You just don't talk that way to other life forms. If they're friendly, it's ungracious; and if they're not friendly... Well! Who knows what they might do?

She could have got us into a whole load of trouble. We could have been vaporised on the spot! As it was, the captain obviously decided to make allowances for her ignorance.

'First of all,' he said, 'allow me to introduce myself. I am Captain Cranko. This is Lieutenant Malandra, and this is Lieutenant Bendra. And this...' He waved a hand. 'Is the command deck of the starship *Galaxy Empire*. We welcome you aboard!'

I knew it, I knew it, I knew it! I *knew* spaceships existed. I knew there were extraterrestrial beings. I *knew* they had transporter beams. I shot a triumphant glance at Rosie. Now let her say it was stupid boy stuff!

Rosie took absolutely no notice at all. She never does when I've proved her wrong. She stood glaring up at the captain, all butch and aggressive.

'If this is some kind of joke,' she said, 'I don't think much of it. I was in the middle of trying to finish my homework when you went and did whatever it is you've gone and done!'

She practically stamped her feet. But the captain just smiled – which made her even madder. I could see she was about to start up again, so I stepped in, hurriedly.

'I was watching *Star Trek*,' I said. I didn't say it to complain; I just wanted to make it clear that *one* of us knew what was going on. 'They were exploring a distant planet, deep in outer space, and Captain Kirk had just asked Scotty to beam him up.'

'A wise man.' Captain Cranko nodded. 'Lieutenant Malandra here is our transporter chief. She has often come to my rescue.'

Lieutenant Malandra did the hand thing, palm up. Obviously a kind of greeting. 'I trust,' she said, 'your journey was a smooth one?'

I assured her that it was. 'I didn't feel a thing, except it was a bit weird seeing my body parts.'

'I agree,' said Lieutenant Malandra. 'It takes a while to grow used to it. I remember my first time, three of my feet —' She stopped, abruptly. If she'd been human, I'm sure she would have blushed. But now I knew for sure she wasn't! *Three* of her feet… How many did she have?

Rosie was making impatient huffing noises, blowing through her mouth. 'It *is* a joke, right?'

'Wrong, I'm afraid.' The captain shook his head. I found myself wondering if it was his only head, or if, like Lieutenant Malandra and her feet, he had several of them. 'We are on an extremely serious mission.'

Rosie's chin tilted. 'So what's it to do with us?' she said.

'Everything! As you shall hear. Meanwhile…' He turned, gravely, to me. 'I regret pulling you away in the middle of your *Star Trek*, but it will be there waiting for you when you get back. You will find Captain Kirk just as you left him, preparing to beam up. I give you my word! Nothing will have changed.'

'How come?' said Rosie.

'Let us just say that … time has temporarily come to a halt. So, please! There is no need to worry.'

I hastened to make it clear that I, personally, wasn't in the least bit worried.

'Well, you mightn't be,' said Rosie. 'I am! It means my homework'll still be there, as well. I could have finished it by now, if you hadn't...'

Her voice trailed off. Her eyes slowly grew as big as satellite dishes. Her jaw dropped, taking her mouth with it. She gobbled a bit, but no words came out. Just a sort of strangled cry. '*Hahhhhhaahaaargh...*'

I turned to see what the problem was – and my jaw dropped as well. I have to admit it. It's best to be truthful about these things. I didn't make the *hahhhhaa* sound, but that was only because I'd clamped a hand to my mouth.

One of the walls had silently gone into meltdown, and a creature had come slithering in. It was all head and tentacles. Big purple head and long green fronds, coiling and writhing. Come to think of it, rather like the octopus thing we'd just seen on *Star Trek*.

What was a bit worrying was that I couldn't remember whether the octopus thing had been deadly, or whether it had simply wanted to shake tentacles. Did Captain Kirk get beamed up in time? Or did the octopus thing get him?

For a minute, I was close to panic. But Captain Kirk never panicked, and neither would I. *In the face of danger, remain calm.* I drew myself up, very stiff and straight. I wasn't going to be terrorised by some octopus thing!

Slowly, it started to coil its way through the door. One of its tentacles, not looking where it was going, touched the edge of Rosie's foot and instantly drew back. Rosie screeched. Long and loud. She clutched at my arm. What was the matter with her? The thing hadn't done her any harm! It was just a different life form. Nothing to be scared of. All the same, it gave me a lot of satisfaction. *Now* let her say that aliens didn't exist!

Chapter Three

As the octopus thing coiled back on itself, away from Rosie's foot, the captain stepped forward. Very coldly he said, 'Zzexxxbjaaarx!' Or something like that. It obviously made sense to the octopus thing. Even though it was an octopus thing, you could tell it was ashamed of itself. Its tentacles began to twist and turn, curling up at the ends like my toes do when I get into trouble.

'Xxozzaaaz!' barked the captain. Or maybe it was 'Zzoxxaaax.' Whichever, it sounded painful. Like he was clearing razor blades out of his throat.

The poor old octopus thing turned bright purple. I mean, it already was purple; but sort of pale. More lavender coloured. Now it looked like a big ripe mulberry. Like it might burst at any minute.

Slowly, starting at the tips of its tentacles, it began to shrivel. As the tentacles shrivelled, the big purple mulberry began to swell, until it was the size of a football. The size of a beach ball. And still growing!

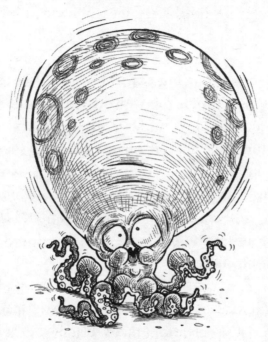

I held my breath, waiting for the explosion. Bracing myself for the *splat* of purple innards landing on my face. But then, quite suddenly, the octopus thing disappeared in a shimmer of light, and in its place stood what appeared to be a normal human being. I knew, of course, that it wasn't really human; it was the octopus thing in disguise.

The captain cleared a few more razor blades out of his throat. 'Graarx orx!' he barked.

The octopus thing snapped to attention. It was wearing the black tracksuit with the logo. The logo was blue, but without any stripes. Must be very junior, I thought. It stood, head bowed before the captain, and earnestly spoke in octopus language. Well, what I took to be octopus language. It didn't sound like razor blades. More like blobs of jelly. Whatever it was, it obviously didn't impress the captain. He snapped, 'Zzexxxgraaach!' and pointed sternly in our direction. The octopus thing swivelled round to face us. Captain Cranko pressed the button on his logo.

'Ensign Gork,' he said, 'wishes to apologise.'

Ensign Gork bent low before us. 'I deeply regret,' he said, 'my thoughtless behaviour. I had not realised there were visitors aboard. But that is no excuse,' he added. 'I am truly sorry for any distress I may have caused.'

'So I should think,' said Rosie, crossly. 'Coming in looking like something that's been fished out of the ocean!'

I kicked at her. Ensign Gork couldn't help looking like an octopus. It was probably quite normal, in his world. He might even have been thought handsome. And what was her problem with octopuses anyway?

The trouble with Rosie is that she never knows when to stop.

'A joke is a joke,' she grumbled, 'but this is ridiculous!'

Poor Ensign Gork had gone bright purple. I thought for a minute he was going to lose control of his cloak and turn back into an octopus. I felt quite embarrassed for him, so I hastily said that he hadn't caused any distress at all. Not as far as I was concerned. Earnestly, I explained how I was quite used to seeing extraterrestrial beings.

'We can't all look alike. I mean, the galaxy would be a pretty dull place if we did!' I gave this little laugh to show how much the idea amused me, all of us looking alike. 'In any case,' I said, 'us lot that live on Earth probably look just as –'

I stopped. Just as what? Just as odd? Just as scary?

'We don't look like octopuses!' shrilled Rosie.

'No.' The captain smiled, kindly. 'You are mainly sacks of water.'

Well, *that* put her in her place. Rosie's mouth

fell open and she popped her eyes; lost for words, for once in her life.

'Please.' The captain held out a hand. 'Step this way. Let me take you somewhere more comfortable where we can talk.'

''bout time,' muttered Rosie; but at least she kept it under her breath.

We followed the captain into the turbo lift. Well, *I* followed the captain. Rosie hesitated.

'What's this?' she said, all aggressive.

I told her it was a turbo lift and she said, 'Oh, yeah?'

'It's all right,' I said. 'It's quite safe. They use them all the time in *Star Trek.*'

Rosie gave me this withering look. 'Know what?' she said. 'You're not safe to be let out! You'd believe anything.'

'No, Rosie, Jake is absolutely right.' The captain spoke in soothing tones, putting his hand under her elbow to encourage her. 'It's perfectly safe. You have nothing to fear.'

I think it shook her a bit, the captain knowing our names. I was a bit surprised, myself, but I tried not to show it. After all, creatures from other planets are not the same as us. They have abilities we don't always understand. Of course, Rosie didn't believe there were creatures from other planets. I could see that must be making things a bit difficult for her. She plainly couldn't understand what was going on.

'Rosie?' The captain waved her forward. 'Please don't be scared. We mean you no harm.'

She shook her head, like *this is too much*. But quite meekly she stepped into the lift beside me. She didn't even say *oh, yeah*?

'Right! Off we go.'

The captain touched a panel of lights and I felt us moving, swift and silent, towards the top of the ship. Rosie jabbed a sudden finger in my ribs. I sprang round, indignantly.

'What d'you do that for?'

She mouthed at me, furiously. 'What's going on? What have you got us into?'

Me? I hadn't got us into anything! I mouthed back that I had no more idea than she did. 'Why blame me?'

Her lips moved, in angry silence. 'You're the one who keeps on about aliens!'

So what? Did she think I'd been sending secret messages, or something? *Please come and abduct us*?

The lips were still moving. 'How'd he know our names? How'd he know where to find us?' But the lift had come to a standstill and the doors were sliding open.

'Jake? Rosie?' The captain stood aside to let us out. 'If you'll come this way.'

He led us into a circular space, a sort of star dome covered in green glass, through which shone an alien sky filled with alien planets which glinted gold and darted like fish through the darkness.

The dome was empty, but at a touch from the captain a circlet of chairs rose from the floor, humping upwards like mushrooms.

The captain gestured to us to take a seat, and obediently I lowered myself into one of the chairs. It felt soft and spongy, like sinking into a marshmallow. Comfortable, though. I couldn't help thinking how my nan would like one. She's always complaining about there being nowhere for her to rest her aching bones.

Rosie stood watching. She said afterwards that she'd been waiting to make sure the thing didn't suddenly turn vicious.

'Could have swallowed you up, or smothered you!'

I told her quite sharply to sit down. It wasn't polite to remain standing when you were someone's guest and they'd provided special seats for you. I wondered what seats, if any, the captain would provide for himself when he wasn't cloaked in human form. Was he another octopus thing? Would he even need a seat?

Rosie, still suspicious, perched herself on the extreme edge of one of the marshmallows. I saw the expression on her face change as she sank down into its softness. Reluctantly, she gave a little grunt of pleasure. I don't think she wanted to; she just couldn't help it.

'Well, now,' said the captain. 'You must be wondering why you've been brought here. I expect you're thinking it's high time I explained…'

Chapter Four

Rosie opened her mouth. I just knew she was going to say something that would make me cringe. Unfortunately, my marshmallow wasn't close enough for me to kick her, so I did the next best thing and jumped in before she could get started.

'Please don't feel you have to rush,' I said. 'We're not in any hurry.'

'What are you talking about?' screeched Rosie. 'I need to get back and finish my homework!'

'You've got the rest of the evening,' I said. 'Time's going to be the same when we get back as it was when we left.' The captain had already told us that. Didn't she listen to a word anyone said? 'We could be here for days, and Mum and Dad wouldn't miss us! They wouldn't even know we'd gone. Isn't that right?' I turned to the captain for confirmation. 'Sir,' I added.

The look Rosie gave me, you'd have thought

I was something that had been brought in on the bottom of a shoe. Her lip curled.

'I'm not staying here for *days*! You can, if you want. I'm going home!"

'Dunno how you think you're going to get there,' I said. 'Not without someone to transport you.'

'You will both be going home,' said the captain. 'Have no fears about that.'

I assured him I had no fears. 'It's just her,' I said. 'She always thinks I'm imagining things – spaceships. Aliens. I mean…' I corrected myself, hastily, not wanting to give offence. Rosie had already been quite rude enough for both of us. 'Different life forms. She thinks you're just made up. Just stupid boy stuff.'

Rosie glared at me.

'It's true,' I said. 'You do nothing but sit there and jeer!'

'It's perfectly understandable,' said the captain. 'Rosie is obviously one of those people who needs to see with her own eyes. So here you are!' He waved a hand. 'All the evidence you need … we really do exist!'

Rosie frowned, like even now she wasn't ready to give in and admit it was all happening.

What would it take to convince her?

The captain sank down into a marshmallow. 'Let me start by telling you something about us. We're a spaceship, as you call them … the *Galactic Empire*. We have a crew made up of nearly thirty different species. Most, including myself, come from planets that are quite unknown to people on Earth. We'd –'

''Scuse me,' said Rosie. 'Can I ask a question?'

'By all means. Go ahead!'

'If you're all from different planets, how come you don't all look different?'

'Well, in our natural forms, of course, we do.'

'So why hide it?' said Rosie.

Why couldn't she just *keep quiet*? If only there were some way of moving my marshmallow to get me within kicking distance!

'What I'm saying,' said Rosie, 'is why not appear in your true colours? Seems a bit of a cheat, if you ask me.'

Was there *no* way to silence her? She was lucky the captain was so patient.

'Please don't get the idea that anyone is seeking to deceive you,' he said. 'We simply wish to put you at your ease. It seems only polite to assume the same form as one's visitors, at least to begin with. I noticed that you were quite alarmed when Ensign Gork failed to cloak himself.'

'That's 'cos he looked like an octopus!'

'Pardon me,' I said, 'but if we were on *his* planet they'd probably think you looked like a blob.'

'Yeah, and they'd think *you* looked like an elephant, with those great ears!'

'I doubt it,' said the captain. 'On most of our planets the inhabitants are quite accustomed to seeing those from other worlds. It's true that few have ever actually encountered an Earthling, but they would not find you in any way peculiar. They know that lives take many different shapes and forms.'

Well! That put her in her place. For about two seconds.

'Let us continue,' said the captain. 'The *Galactic Empire* is one of several spaceships on patrol throughout the galaxy. We are part of an organisation known as Planetary Investigation and Exploration – PIE, for short.'

He indicated the initials on his shoulder flash … PIE. Rosie looked, and let out a snort.

'Pie in the sky!'

There was a pause, during which I seriously thought of getting up and clobbering her. The captain seemed puzzled.

'I'm sorry,' he said, 'my translator…' He tapped the button in the middle of his logo. 'Appears not to have come across this expression. Does it have some significance?'

Rosie gurgled, happily. 'It's what our dad says when he finds something just, like, totally *un-be-lievable* – pie in the sky!'

'Interesting.' The captain nodded gravely. 'I must have it programmed in. Thank you for instructing me.'

'You're welcome,' said Rosie, with a little annoying smirk.

This time I didn't just want to clobber, I wanted to *throttle*. She wasn't usually this bad. Mum sometimes accuses her of being a smart-mouth, and once she was told off for talking back to a teacher, but that's because she just can't seem to control herself. What I mean is, she doesn't normally go out of her way to be insulting. But I couldn't just sit back and let her carry on. She was giving Earth a bad name!

I edged forward on my marshmallow. Earnestly, I addressed the captain. 'If it's not top secret, or anything, could we hear more about what you do? I happen to be extremely interested,' I said, 'in learning about space travel. I've done a lot of research on the subject.'

'I am aware of that.' The captain smiled. 'It's one of the reasons we chose you.'

Chose me? So it wasn't just random. I'd been chosen! I couldn't help shooting a look of triumph at Rosie. Not that she took any notice;

she never does. Instead, she had the nerve to turn to the captain and say, 'Chosen us for what? Exactly?'

I'd have laughed if she hadn't been my sister, giving Earth a bad name. She really thought *she'd* been chosen? Who'd want her? Most likely she'd just been picked up by accident when I was beamed aboard. Some kind of transporter malfunction. These things happened.

'We shall come to that in a moment,' said the captain. 'First, let me explain what brings us to this particular corner of the galaxy. We are here on a mission to hunt down members of an inter-planetary terrorist organisation, which goes under the name of SLADE – the Secret League of Alien Destroyers. You will no doubt find it difficult to believe, but aliens have been on your planet for decades.'

I knew it, I knew it! I'd known it all along.

'Many of them,' continued the captain, 'have actually taken up residence.'

'What, on Earth?' said Rosie, in her *oh, yeah?* voice.

'Absolutely! It's quite commonplace. They are scattered across all four quarters of your globe. There can be very few people who haven't come into contact with one at some time or another – without, of course, realising. They keep themselves very carefully cloaked.'

'Guess they would,' said Rosie. 'Octopuses walking down the road'd be a dead giveaway!'

'Excuse me.' I turned on her, irritably. 'Some of us are trying to hold a serious conversation here.'

'Oh, yeah?'

'Yeah!'

'So what'll it be next? Lobsters playing football?'

She hooted, happily, at her own turn of wit. I informed her, somewhat coldly, that it was no laughing matter.

'Speak for yourself. I think it's hilarious!'

Rosie fell back into her marshmallow, clutching her stomach. I looked across at the captain, and shook my head.

'I apologise for my sister,' I said.

A venomous hiss came from Rosie's marshmallow. 'Creep!'

'I've always known there's aliens,' I said. The word had slipped out before I could stop it. I felt my cheeks turn pink, and hurried on. 'I reckon we've got one in our school.'

'Probably got a whole lot,' said Rosie. 'Most of the boys in Year 6, for a start.'

'Let us see.' The captain tapped a finger to his wrist and a computer screen suddenly lit up the far wall. How had he done that? Must be some kind of gadget he was wearing. Some kind of remote control. 'Blythe Bridge Middle School, Year 6.'

My year. And there we all were, on the screen.

'No! No aliens in Year 6,' said the captain.

'Try Year 7,' I suggested. Year 7 was *her* year. What a laugh if my sister turned out to be one! But the captain said there were no aliens in Year 7, either.

'What about the teachers?' I said. 'Mrs Openshaw … I bet she's one!'

A picture of the teachers appeared, with Mrs Openshaw standing grimly in their midst.

'Mrs Openshaw is fully human,' said the captain. 'But that one … Miss Simkins. She's an Argosian. Comes from Argos III.'

Miss Simpkins?

'But she's nice!' I said.

'Yes, she's a real sweetie. She's been on Earth for a few years now. Arrived as a child, with her parents. She's one of the ones who've settled in

37

really well. A lot never make it. Most return to their own planets within the first year. A few stay on and turn to petty crime. One or two even end up in your prisons. The vast majority, however, are perfectly harmless, just trying to get on with their lives. They go about their daily business, without you ever noticing. They're not the ones we're after. The ones we're after are the ones that SLADE manage to slip through the net. They can be real troublemakers. And that,' said the captain, turning back to face us, 'is where we need your help...'

Chapter Five

Wow! I sat up straighter on my marshmallow. This was serious stuff. The Planetary Investigation and Exploration service needed my help!

'I am very much hoping,' said the captain, 'that our appeal will not fall on deaf ears.'

No way!

'I'll do anything you want,' I said.

'Hang about, hang about!' Rosie flapped a hand. 'What exactly,' she said to the captain, 'did you have in mind? 'Cos if it's rounding up octopuses, it's not really my sort of thing. In any case, like I said, I have to be getting back. It's all very well you keeping on about how time is at a standstill, but I've still got my homework to do. It's OK for *him*.' She jerked her head in my direction. 'He's only Year 6. He doesn't have any. I've got a whole load!'

Yes, and as far as I was concerned, they could send her straight back to get on with it. I couldn't imagine what help they thought she was likely to be. She didn't even believe in them!

'Let me explain the situation,' said the captain. 'See if I can persuade you. It's not so much a question of *rounding up octopuses*, as you put it. More a question of rooting out an alien bug.'

Rosie jutted her chin. 'What sort of bug?'

'An extremely unpleasant sort. One of the most dangerous. It comes from a planet way out on the extreme edge of the galaxy. Not a great deal is known about it, but it's recently come to our attention that SLADE have been recruiting there, and we think they may have managed to smuggle in quite a few of these exceptionally nasty creatures. So far we've located up to a hundred, spread across the globe. There may be more; we're hoping not.'

'So what exactly do they do?' said Rosie.

'They … take up residence,' said the captain.

'What, like woodworm, or something?' Our dad had once discovered woodworm in an old piece of furniture. He'd shown us all the holes they'd made. Then he'd chopped up the furniture and made a bonfire of it. 'Woodworm are deadly,' said Rosie. She sounded quite proud of the fact. Who needed alien bugs when we had bugs of our own?

'Believe me,' said the captain, 'woodworm do not even begin to compare. Woodworm only destroy property. These things go for people.'

'*Oo-er*,' said Rosie. She shivered, dramatically. 'Save me!'

She still wasn't taking it seriously. I was! I knew from *Star Trek* that there were all kinds of vicious bugs out there, just waiting to get at us.

'How big are they?' I said. I once saw this movie where they had beetles the size of horses. That had been pretty scary.

'They're not actually very big at all,' said the captain. 'Quite small, in fact. The danger does not lie in their size – except, of course, it means they can move around without drawing attention to themselves. People simply don't notice them until it's too late. I suppose they could best be likened to one of your Earth insects ... the centipede? Let me show you.'

The captain tapped something into the gadget on his wrist and this creature appeared on the computer screen. It was long and brown and shiny, like a centipede with an outsize head, on either side of which were vicious–looking fangs. Its legs, wriggling and kicking, were covered in sharp spikes.

'Not a pretty picture, I think you will agree.'
The captain tapped again, and we saw the same
creature in close-up. It had big bulging eyes and
two small horns sticking out the top of its head,
and I saw that its fangs were dripping with what
looked like yellow pus.

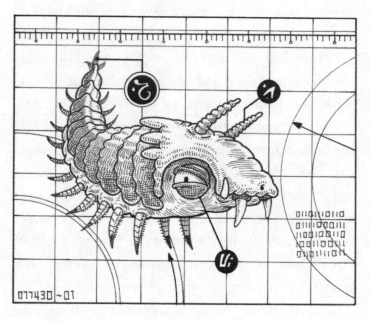

'Poison,' said the captain.

Rosie made a sound like she was going to be
sick. Even I recoiled slightly. But I quickly
pulled myself together. *Never show fear.* It was
only a bug, and a small one at that.

'Looks like it'd be pretty easy to crush,' I said.

'I bet if you stamped on it, it'd go splat.'

'Oh, it would certainly go splat,' said the captain. 'If, that is, you managed to stamp on it before it ran up your leg and disappeared.'

There was a pause. I looked at Rosie. Rosie looked at me. Why didn't she say something? She was the one that liked to do all the talking! But Rosie pulled a face, like, *go on, then*! I cleared my throat.

'W-w-where would it d-d-disappear to?'

'Inside you,' said the captain. 'First they sink in their fangs, then they burrow. You probably wouldn't even be aware it was happening. When the fangs pierce the skin, it has a deadening effect. Once inside, they head for the brain, and that's it. To all intents and purpose, you become their slave.'

'That sounds good,' said Rosie. 'Slave to a bug!'

All very well, her sounding so jaunty. She'd be the first to scream if she saw one. She nearly has hysterics if a spider walks across the ceiling.

'The fact is,' said the captain, 'once these bugs have dug themselves in, they can force you to do whatever they want. Start wars, destroy businesses, just generally cause havoc. It's their whole reason for being on Earth – to wipe out the population and take over the planet. This is why it's so vitally important that they should be rooted out.'

'And you want us to do the rooting?' said Rosie. 'I don't think so!'

'Surely there's got to be some kind of treatment?' I said. 'Some kind of tablet people could take? That's what happened when our cat had worms, we gave her tablets and then she was all right. They're probably working on it right now.'

'I wish it were the case,' said the captain. 'Unfortunately it's not. Apart from anything else, no one on your world realises that these bugs exist. Not even those who have been taken over by them.'

'So… How d'you get rid of them? You don't have to *kill* people?' I said.

'No, no!' The captain sounded quite shocked. 'The aim is to destroy the bugs, not the people.'

'And that's what you want us to do,' said Rosie. She gave a little snort of laughter. 'Like we're the SAS, or something.'

I wouldn't actually mind being in the SAS. It is in fact my second ambition, my first one being to join the space programme.

'Rest assured,' said the captain, 'the only violence will be to the bugs. Once they have been eliminated, the people quickly return to their normal selves. They don't even remember being taken over.'

'And you know this how?' said Rosie.

'Trust me,' said the captain. 'I speak from experience. This is far from being our first mission. We have been patrolling this part of the galaxy for over a decade – ever since the bugs started arriving. We know all their nasty little habits. They're mean, they're vicious, and they have to be stopped!'

'Hmm.' Rosie looked at him with narrowed eyes. 'How can you tell when a person's been taken over?'

'There are signs. Sudden unexplained changes in behaviour, for example. We keep a close look out. We are constantly checking your news bulletins, computer blogs, anything which might alert us to the possibility.'

'But how can you actually *tell*?'

Rosie really knows how to keep at it. But I was quite interested in hearing the answer myself.

'We observe,' said the captain. 'We investigate. It's not always easy. In some cases, it can take several months before we know for sure.'

'You still haven't said *how*,' objected Rosie. She was starting to sound a bit querulous. 'I mean, someone could just be going mad, in a quite ordinary sort of way. How do you know they're not just going ordinarily mad?'

'What it comes down to, in the end, is finding physical evidence. Let me show you.'

The captain tapped again on his wrist, and the back of someone's head appeared on the screen. Someone with long blond hair covering their neck.

'Watch,' said the captain. We watched, as a hand snaked across the screen and carefully scooped the hair out of the way. 'You see that?' He pointed at a tiny red mark on the back of the neck. 'That's the evidence we look for. Let me magnify it.'

The tiny red mark suddenly became a gaping hole, in the middle of which could be seen the wriggling legs of one of the centipede things. It made me feel peculiar, just looking at it.

'That,' said the captain, 'is one we managed to catch as it was burrowing its way in. Nasty little blighters, I think you'll agree.'

I saw Rosie's hand go up to feel her neck. She caught me watching her and immediately pretended to be fiddling with her hair.

'Out of interest,' said the captain, 'you might care to see a few of the people we know for sure have been taken over. For instance...'

A face flashed up on the screen. Blimey! I recognised it as belonging to an MP that Dad particularly hated. Every time the MP opened his mouth, Dad went ballistic and started shouting that the man was an idiot. Now I knew why. He'd been taken over by a bug!

Another face came up.

'That's Pete Sullivan!' Rosie sounded outraged. Pete Sullivan was, like, her all-time favourite singer. He was with this band called Death Metal that Mum didn't like her listening to 'cos she said they were too violent.

And great galloping grandmothers! That was the face of someone I'd seen on the telly. He'd just been chucked out for using bad language in front of half a million viewers.

Oh, and that was the lady that was so mean to all the people that came on her show. Only last week she'd made someone cry.

Different faces flashed on and off the screen. Some were famous. Some I didn't know. But all of them, said the captain, had been taken over by bugs. And then…

Then it happened.

I catapulted backwards on my marshmallow. Rosie practically jumped right out of hers.

'I thought that would get your attention,' said the captain.

Chapter Six

I could feel my jaw dropping, and my mouth hanging open.

'It's the Queen!' The words came out in a kind of yelp. Was the captain really saying that the *Queen* had been taken over?

Rosie was hugging herself, rocking to and fro. 'Now I've heard everything … the Queen's got a bug!'

'She can't have,' I said. There had to be some mistake. Bugs in Buckingham Palace? 'How would it get past security?'

'All too easily,' said the captain. 'It's more surprising how it got past the corgis. We're working on the theory that they swamped the place with suicide bugs in the hope that just one would manage to get through without being eaten.'

'Oh, I love this,' said Rosie. 'I love it, I love it!'

I turned, rather desperately, to the captain.

If even the Queen had been bugged, what hope was there for the rest of us?

'As of this moment,' said the captain, 'we don't actually have any definite proof. But take it from me, we're ninety-nine per cent certain. We've been keeping a very careful eye on her recent behaviour. You may remember, a few months ago, that the Queen was in a health scare? She had to cancel her engagements?'

I nodded, doubtfully.

'I remember,' said Rosie. 'Mum said it wasn't like her, but it was only to be expected 'cos, after all, she was getting on a bit.'

'In human terms,' said the captain, 'that is correct. The inhabitants of your planet do have extraordinarily short life spans. This, of course, is why you're still so backward … you simply don't live long enough to learn.'

I could see Rosie start to bristle.

'It's not your fault,' said the captain, soothingly. 'Your planet is still in its infancy. You have a lot of growing up to do. But yes, your mother is quite right, the Queen is no longer young and it is not surprising if she suffers the occasional ailment. On this occasion, however, there was nothing wrong whatsoever.

You may be interested to learn that she spent three whole days sitting in bed playing computer games and eating what I believe you refer to as junk food – burgers and chips, and chicken nuggets?'

I stared, goggle-eyed. The *Queen*? Eating chicken nuggets? In her *bedroom*?

Rosie gave one of her shrill shrieks of laughter. The sort that makes Dad clap his hands to his ears. 'Sounds a lot more fun than going round factories!'

'Yes; the bug obviously thought so. Just as last week it thought it would be fun to throw bread rolls at a banquet given for the Russian president.'

'We never heard about that,' I said.

'You wouldn't. The Palace kept it very quiet.'

'Maybe she's just going loopy,' said Rosie. 'People do, when they get old.'

'Trust me,' said the captain. 'She is not going loopy. She's been invaded by a bug, and it has to be removed. This is where you come in. You and Jake. We should like to recruit you as honorary members of PIE.'

'What's that mean?' said Rosie. 'Honorary members?'

'It means you have been specially chosen to help defend your planet. We can't offer you full membership, I'm afraid; Earth is not yet advanced enough to qualify. But you would be part of a very select band.'

'Why us?'

Why *her*, more to the point. I still didn't see what use anyone thought she was going to be.

'Why can't you do it yourselves?' said Rosie. 'Seeing as you're so advanced.'

'The fact is,' said the captain, 'the entire galaxy is under threat. It is essential that we all work together. Unfortunately, we are not permitted to land on any planet that is not a member of PIE. This is for a good reason. You may think of us as … what was it? Perambulating octopuses?'

'That was her,' I said. 'Not me!'

I was glad to see Rosie's cheeks turn pink. She wasn't *totally* without shame.

'Octopuses, centipedes … we take many shapes and forms. But we all belong to worlds that are technologically far in advance of Earth. For us to land on your planet would be disastrous. It would not only cause havoc, but far worse, it would contaminate the time line.'

I'd heard about the time line. I wasn't quite sure what it was, but I knew it was very important not to contaminate it.

'You see,' said the captain, 'we are actually part of the future.'

Yesss! I punched the air, exultantly. Now I understood.

Rosie, obviously, still didn't.

'So, if you're from the future,' she said, 'why not just put things right and then move on?'

Shocked, I said, ''Cos people from the future mustn't ever interfere with the past! It's one of the rules.'

'It's why we have to recruit local agents,' explained the captain. 'It's why we've recruited you. Or hope to recruit you. We've had you under observation for some while. Jake, because he's eager to find out as much as he can about space travel.' I swelled, importantly. 'We always watch out for those who show an interest.'

'*I* didn't show any interest,' said Rosie.

'No, but you are quick to learn. You are very much the type we like to recruit.'

Pardon me???

'You ask questions, you demand answers, you don't let anyone push you around. Plus, of course, we are aware that you have already looked death in the face.'

Oh, please! Not that again. I was sick of hearing how Rosie had looked death in the face. All it was, she'd read this book where a kid climbed out of the bedroom window and slid down the drainpipe, so she thought she'd try doing it, too, only she went and got stuck halfway down and was there for nearly an hour before she was discovered. Dad had to get a ladder and rescue her. She'd been on about it ever since. How she'd looked death in the face.

'And didn't panic!'

Rosie smirked.

'I won't pretend,' said the captain, 'that the mission would be without danger. These bugs are vicious, and they move at great speed. You would need to move at even greater speed. It would be a question of dislodging the creature from the Queen, then zapping it before it could attack one of you. I can give you no guarantee that this would not happen. I can only assure you that if it did we would take immediate action. We would not abandon you to your fate.'

There was a bit of a pause, while I wondered what exactly our fate would be. I shot a glance at Rosie.

'Yeah. Well! Yeah.' She bounced on her marshmallow. 'OK, then!'

What did she mean, *OK then*?

'Let's go for it!'

Really? I stared at her, gobsmacked.

'Jake?' said the captain. 'How about you?'

'Oh, he'll do it,' said Rosie. 'He's been waiting for something like this for years.'

It was true, I had; but I didn't see what right she had to speak for me. She has this really annoying habit of just taking over.

'So, what's the plan?' she said.

'The plan,' said the captain, 'is that we send you back home and you wait for us to contact you. Probably in the next twenty-four hours. Earth hours, that is.'

Rosie nodded. 'OK.'

'Got it,' I said, feeling it was time I re-entered the conversation.

'I'd better let you have a communicator. Jake, here, you take it.'

A com badge. He'd actually given me a com badge!

'I would just ask you not to use it unless you're in trouble. I know I can trust you.' I swallowed, and nodded. Rosie curled her lip. 'As soon as you hear from us, expect to be beamed up and given your instructions. In the meantime –'

'I know!' Rosie zipped a finger across her mouth. 'Say nothing to anyone. My lips are sealed!'

'No need for that,' said the captain. 'Feel free to say whatever you like! The very reason we use children as our agents is that no one ever believes them. Try telling your mum and dad you've been abducted by aliens … what do you think they're likely to do?'

'Yeah, right,' said Rosie. 'I see what you mean.'

'They do have these stories in the papers,' I said. 'People being abducted.'

'Yes.' The captain frowned. 'That's because we made the mistake, in the past, of using adults. It took us a while to realise that children were far better, from a security point of view.'

'Not that it really matters,' said Rosie. 'No one actually believes in aliens … only nutters!'

Chapter Seven

'Guess what?' said Rosie. 'I've just had the weirdest dream! I dreamt we'd been abducted by aliens.' It obviously embarrassed her. '*Me*!' She gave this little titter, to show how ridiculous it was. 'Dreaming about aliens! Can you imagine?'

I said, 'I don't have to imagine. I was there.'

'I know you were there! I just told you … they abducted *us*. In a spaceship! That's what comes of trying to do my homework while you're watching that rubbish.' She waved a hand at the television, where *Star Trek* was still going on – right at the point where we'd left it. 'There was this thing,' said Rosie, 'like an octopus –'

'Ensign Gork.'

'What?' She looked at me, eyes narrowed.

'Ensign Gork. That's what he was called.'

'How do you know what he was called?'

''Cos I was there,' I reminded her.

'In my dream! *My* dream.' Rosie stabbed a

finger at herself. 'Not your dream: *my* dream. People can't share dreams!'

'So how come I know his name?'

She pursed her lips, trying to think up an answer.

'And how come…' I slid my hand into the pocket of my jeans and pulled out something small and round and silver. 'How come I've got this?'

Rosie stared. It was the com badge the captain had given me. Rosie had seen him do it. How was she going to wriggle out of that one?

For a moment I thought she was going to admit, just for once, that I was right and she was wrong. But Rosie never gives in without a fight.

'You don't think it actually *works*?' she said, scornfully. 'Probably some kind of stupid toy.'

'Doesn't explain how it got in my pocket.'

She chewed at her lip. 'See what happens if you press the button.'

'No, I can't. You heard the captain … we're not to use it unless we're in trouble.'

'Who's he to go giving orders? Him and his aliens… *Queen's got a bug*!' Rosie gave one of her uncouth cackles. 'Pardon me while I die laughing!'

'Look at the time,' I said.

'Why?' She shot a quick glance at the clock. 'What's that got to do with anything?'

'The captain told us it'd stand still.'

'Clock's obviously stopped.'

'The clock hasn't stopped,' I said. 'Time is what stopped.' I couldn't expect her to understand. 'Temporal mechanics are extremely complicated. You'd know, if you watched *Star Trek*. Time can do almost anything. Go backwards, go forwards. Go fast, go slow. Did you know, for instance, that if you travelled far enough into space you could come back to Earth only a few months older than when you left, while everyone else would have grown old and died?'

'Oh, you'd swallow any old rubbish!' said Rosie.

'OK.' I waved the com badge at her. 'So what's your explanation? Are you telling me you don't believe what just happened?'

Rosie hooked her hair behind her ears. 'Obviously *something* happened. It's a question of what. Probably some kind of … government experiment. Something to do with carbon emissions. A new kind of transport!' She pounced on the idea, triumphantly. 'They're going to get rid of cars and planes and all those stinky things that are manking up the planet and we're all going to whiz around in beams of light. But obviously it's top secret, they're still trying it out. *That's* why they're using kids! 'Cos like they said, nobody'd believe us.'

I gazed at her, doubtfully. Could she be right?

'The government wouldn't abduct *children*,' I said.

'Governments'd do anything,' said Rosie.

'But what about Ensign Gork? How'd they get someone to look like an octopus?'

'Easy! They do it all the time in movies.'

'But what would be the point?'

'Put you off the scent. Make you think there's aliens.'

'There *are* aliens. Except,' I remembered, 'it's not polite to call them that.'

'*He* did.'

'If you mean the captain –'

'Captain!' Rosie snorted. 'Government agent, more like.'

'If he was a government agent,' I said, 'he ought to know better. If he was the captain…' Which he was. I knew he was! 'Well, he's allowed to say it, 'cos he is one.'

'One what?'

'Alien. Different life form! It's like people with red hair can call themselves Carrots if they want, but not anyone else.'

'Who says?'

'It's a known fact,' I said. 'It's rude. Might hurt their feelings. Like you calling me Elephant Ears.'

'You *are* Elephant Ears.'

'Yeah, well, in that case you're the Blob!'

'Oh, shut up,' snapped Rosie. 'I've had enough interruption for one evening.' She went back to her laptop, fiercely clacking and clattering and frowning at the screen. 'Wonder if the newspapers'd be interested? Might pay us something – **SCHOOLCHILDREN ABDUCTED BY ALIENS!**'

'Thought you said it was government agents?'

'Yeah, but that doesn't sound so good,' said Rosie. 'Anyway, they probably wouldn't be allowed to print it. Not if it's the government. Might come and take us away.'

'But we haven't *done* anything,' I said.

'So what? Wouldn't stop them liquidating us.'

Liquidating … the word rolled round my

brain. I had visions of me and Rosie being stuffed headfirst into giant food processors and coming out the other end as juice.

'Like oranges,' I said.

'What?'

'Being liquidated.'

'That's liquid*ised*! Liquidating means bumping off. Tied into sacks and dumped over the side of a boat, most like. Either that, or chucked off the top of a tower block ... squish! Then you *would* be liquidised!'

For some reason, she seemed to find this amusing. She has a very odd sense of humour.

'I still reckon it was aliens,' I said. I'd given up calling them *different life forms*. It was too much trouble, and Rosie took no notice anyway. 'Stands to reason we can't be the only things in the universe.'

'Yeah, way to go,' said Rosie.

Whatever that was supposed to mean. She doesn't always make sense.

It was at this moment that Mum came in. 'Rosie, I've told you before,' she said. 'If you're doing homework, you should be up in your room. How can you possibly concentrate with the television on?'

'It's not the television that bothers me,' said Rosie, 'it's being abducted.' She looked up boldly at Mum. 'By government agents,' she said.

'Or aliens,' I said.

'Whatever.' Rosie waved a hand. 'We've only just got back.'

'Right. Good try!' said Mum. 'But I wouldn't make that excuse to your teachers, if I were you.'

'No, 'cos they wouldn't believe me,' said Rosie.

'Just get on with it,' said Mum. 'Either go upstairs, or you, Jake, turn that television off.'

'OK.' I zapped it with the remote. I couldn't concentrate on *Star Trek* any more; not now I'd been in contact with the real thing. 'Mum, d'you remember,' I said, 'when the Queen had to cancel her engagements?'

'Vaguely,' said Mum. 'She had the flu.'

'That's what they *said*,' said Rosie. 'D'you want to hear the truth? Truth is, she was sitting in bed playing computer games.'

'Well, good for her,' said Mum. 'Keeping up with modern technology.'

'She was also eating chicken nuggets,' said Rosie.

I waited with interest to hear Mum's response. Me and Rosie aren't allowed to eat chicken nuggets. But if the *Queen* could eat them…

'Don't push your luck,' said Mum. 'And just get on with that homework. I want it finished by the time your dad gets in.'

Mum left the room. Me and Rosie exchanged glances. Rosie gave me the thumbs up. Mum hadn't believed a single word we'd said.

Chapter Eight

I stayed awake half the night, waiting for a message to come through from the captain. I wasn't exactly *expecting* it, in the middle of the night, but I wanted to be ready when the call came. I hid the com badge under my pillow, where Mum's prying eyes couldn't see it. She has this nasty habit of bursting into my room in the morning, all bright and breezy, yanking back the curtains and tugging at the duvet and shrieking at me to *get up, get up*! I didn't want her zeroing in and asking awkward questions.

'What's this? Where did it come from?'

I decided that if that happened I would simply tell her the truth.

'It's a communicator, Mum. The aliens gave it to us. D'you remember? The ones that abducted us?'

And then she would go, 'Oh, *those* aliens,' and give a little laugh, like humouring me. She'd never think it might be true!

It must have been the early hours before I finally got to sleep, which meant I didn't wake up till really late. But that was OK, 'cos it was Saturday. I yawned my way out onto the landing and bumped into Rosie. She was also yawning.

'I couldn't sleep,' she said accusingly. Like it was my fault.

I told her that I couldn't sleep, either. 'Didn't hardly like to,' I said, 'in case the call came.'

Holding myself in readiness; that's what I'd been doing. Dunno what she'd been doing. Waiting for government agents to come and get her, probably.

'You're not still expecting that stupid yo-yo thing to work?' said Rosie. 'I told you, it's just a toy! They only gave it you to keep you happy. It's —' She broke off abruptly, head tilted to one side. 'What's that? That bleeping noise? Is it the smoke alarm? *Daaaad*!' She ran to the head of the stairs. 'The smoke alarm!'

It wasn't the smoke alarm: it was the com badge, bleeping in my pocket. I pulled it out. Rosie's eyes had gone like saucers.

'Stupid yo-yo thing,' I said. I pressed the button in the centre and a voice came through.

'This is the starship *Galactic Empire*. Lieutenant Malandra calling Acting Ensign Jake McGraw.'

Acting Ensign! My heart swelled. 'Speaking,' I said, then added, 'Sir.'

'Is Acting Ensign Rosie McGraw also there?'

I pulled a face at Rosie. 'Yeah,' I said. 'She's here.'

'Please stand by to beam up. Do you have that, Ensign McGraw?'

I nodded, speechless.

'Confirm, please.'

'I CONFIRM!' In my excitement, I bellowed it. Dad, halfway up the stairs, looked at me in astonishment.

'What's going on? What's this about the smoke alarm?'

'Sorry, made a mistake,' said Rosie. 'It wasn't the alarm, it was the yo-yo thing.'

'Oh. Well! Right. Glad to see you've managed to get yourselves out of bed at last.'

'We have to go out,' I said, following Dad back down the stairs.

'Where're we going?' hissed Rosie.

I mouthed at her. 'You know where we're going... We're beaming back up.'

'In that case…' Rosie put on a spurt, rudely elbowing me to one side and cantering past Dad along the hall. 'I'm not going without my breakfast!'

We stood in the kitchen, shovelling cereal into our mouths.

'Charming,' said Mum, as we guzzled and gulped. 'Do I take it you're in some kind of a rush?'

'Yup.' I shovelled vigorously. 'We gotta go.'

'I'd sooner you didn't choke yourselves.'

'Can't help it.' A spray of cornflakes shot out of Rosie's mouth. Mum ducked. 'It's urgent! They're coming for us any second.'

'Who's coming?' Mum sounded bewildered.

'Aliens,' said Rosie. 'Or government agents. We're not quite sure. But one or the other.'

'Same ones from yesterday,' I said. 'They're beaming us back up.'

'Oh. Well … have a good time,' said Mum. 'Don't forget Auntie Jay and Uncle Kev are coming for lunch. I'd like to think you'd…'

Her voice faded. We were off! Scrambled together in the transporter. I felt that I was an old hand at it by now. It didn't bother me when body parts went whizzing past. I knew what was happening. I knew they'd all come together again in the right order. *Hopefully* in the right order. I'd once seen a movie where someone's ears ended up on top of their head. Still, it seemed a small price to pay. I reckon there's not much to beat the thrill of hurtling through space in a beam of light.

Both Lieutenant Malandra and the captain were waiting for us as we unscrambled. For a wonderful moment, I thought one of Rosie's hands was going to end up sticking out of her knee cap, but it zoomed back into position.

'Welcome back aboard,' said the captain. 'Glad you could make it!'

'Didn't have much choice,' muttered Rosie; but she said it low so only I could hear. Now that she knew she wasn't just dreaming, she was being a bit more careful. Nobody with any sense wants to run the risk of upsetting a bunch of aliens. Or government agents, whichever they turned out to be. Myself, I was pretty sure they were the real thing; I didn't reckon the government had the technology for transporter beams.

'We have no time to waste,' said the captain, 'so let's crack on. We've located the Queen, she's about to sit down for what I believe you call elevenses.'

Rosie wrinkled her nose. 'What's elevenses?'

'The ritual cup of coffee? With the biscuits? It is being brought to her even as we speak, so let me give you a quick briefing and you can be off. Your mission, as explained previously, is to remove an alien bug. In order to achieve that, you will need these.' He handed each of us what looked like a thin silver pen with a click top.

'Neat,' said Rosie. Of course, she couldn't resist clicking, could she? She just had to do it. Trust her! A quivering black tongue shot out of the end of the pen and lashed, angrily, in the air, making little darts back and forth. Rosie went, 'Eek!' and sprang backwards. Served her right! She did manage to hold on, though. To give her her due, as Mum would say.

'That is a needle gun,' said the captain. 'You need to be careful how you handle them. They are deadly to these particular bugs, but they can also give you humanoids a fairly nasty nip.' He took the gun from Rosie and calmly clicked the top. The tongue wriggled its way back in. 'There you are. All safe. The idea is that you will approach the Queen from behind, point the gun and fire. The bug won't be able to get out fast enough. As soon as it's out, give it another shot to finish it off, and that will be that: end of mission. You have your com badge. Just call through to the ship and we shall beam you back up. Any questions?'

My head was teeming with them, but before I could decide which one to ask first, Rosie had gone jumping in ahead of me.

'I'd just like to know,' she said, 'how we're

s'posed to go creeping up behind the Queen's neck without her noticing anything.'

Yes; that had been one of my questions, too.

'Don't worry!' said the captain. 'We'll be downsizing you before you go.'

There was a pause.

'Excuse me?' said Rosie.

'You're going to be reduced,' said the captain. 'Quite considerably.'

Rosie bristled. She is sensitive about her size; she is already quite small enough. Dad sometimes calls her Midget.

'Excuse *me*,' she said, 'I didn't sign up to be made the size of a…' She waved a hand. 'A two year old!'

'Oh, you'll need to be reduced far more than that.' The captain sounded quite cheerful about it. 'Think mouse. Think *pygmy* mouse. Think…' He held up a finger and thumb, a few centimetres apart. 'Think *micro* pygmy mouse. That should do it.'

Rosie's eyes were almost popping out of her head. And now I, too, had a question I needed to ask.

'Yes, Jake,' said the captain. 'What's troubling you?'

73

'I was just wondering,' I said, 'if we're like sort of … mouse size … how do we get around? Like if we're down *here*…' I crouched. 'How do we get up *there*?'

'Good question,' said the captain. 'I'm glad you asked that.'

The answer, of course, was jet packs. I should have thought of that for myself! I was really annoyed I hadn't. We were each given one and shown how to use it.

'I hope you've got that,' I said to Rosie. She is seriously useless when it comes to technology. I didn't want her suddenly propelling herself into the furniture or knocking herself out on the ceiling.

'I think I can tell up from down, thank you very much!' snapped Rosie. '*And* left from right,' she added, 'which is more than you sometimes can.'

'I'm sure you will both manage perfectly well,' said the captain. 'Remember, you are doing your planet a great service. Now, if you would just step into the conversion chamber…'

He indicated a pool of light, which had suddenly appeared. Rosie and I looked at each other.

'Trust me,' said the captain, 'no harm will come to you. I have been downsized more times than I can remember. And Lieutenant Malandra here was once reduced to a mere atom. I assure you, it is standard procedure. As soon as your mission is completed, we shall restore you to full normality. Before you go, you had better take one of these.'

He held out two small bubble packs full of what looked like dog biscuits.

'What's this for?' said Rosie. 'Not supposed to be our lunch, is it?'

'You will be back home well before lunchtime,' the captain assured her. 'These are for the royal corgis. She has four with her at present. Be warned, they will be able to pick up your voices. The Queen will not. To her, you will sound like bat squeaks. The corgis, however, are a different matter. They have been known to chase and devour small creatures, so I would advise you to break open your bubble packs and scatter the contents at the first sign of danger.'

'This sounds like it's going to be fun,' said Rosie.

I think she was being sarcastic; it's hard to tell, with her. She has this really weird sense of humour. We stepped into the beam of light, clutching our bubble packs, and the captain gave the order.

'Two to beam down!'

We were on our way...

Chapter Nine

I'd have thought being mouse-sized would make you feel different. I'd have thought all the bits of fingers and toes floating about in the transporter would have *looked* different. But they didn't; they just looked like ordinary fingers and toes, the way they always did. And I just felt like me, the way I always did. Until we materialised at the other end ... and then it hit me. I was stranded on some kind of ledge, with a sheer drop below. It was like being at the top of a mountain, looking down into a ravine. This was because *I was mouse-size, up near the ceiling.*

Rosie was perched next to me. She was staring, transfixed, into space. I wanted to nudge her, to get her attention, but was terrified that if I did, she would lose her balance and go plummeting over the edge. And being Rosie, and so useless with technology, she almost certainly wouldn't think to activate her jet pack until it was too late. She might be a total pain, but she is my sister. I wouldn't want to watch her go *splat* on whatever lay below.

What *did* lie below? I risked a quick glance, my finger ready on the up button, just in case. From a great way off, I saw the Queen, sitting at a table. I knew it was the Queen 'cos she was wearing her crown. She was slurping coffee from a big mug. I could hear her slurping even at that distance. Mum would have something to say if me and Rosie did that, but being the Queen she was probably allowed.

Now she was picking up a biscuit and dunking it in her coffee. Oh, and now she was holding it up, all wet and flabby, and tipping her head back so she could drop it in her mouth. Oops! Some of it had broken off before she could get it in. A mush of biscuit fell to the floor and instantly a pack of corgis fell on it, snapping and snarling. The Queen laughed. She obviously thought it very funny. Her hand reached out for another biscuit, but instead of dunking it in her coffee she tossed it at the corgis.

I felt a jab in the ribs, and jumped. It was Rosie. I guessed she didn't care if I went plummeting. Or maybe she knew that I would operate my jet pack.

'This is too gross,' she said.

Did she mean gross that the Queen was chucking biscuits about the place? Or gross that we were stuck on a ledge somewhere up near the ceiling?

'What are we supposed to *do*?'

At the sound of her voice, one of the corgis looked up and barked.

'Shut up!' yelled the Queen, and threw another biscuit.

I said, 'You know what we're supposed to do – we're supposed to destroy an alien bug.'

'I don't want to destroy an alien bug,' said Rosie. 'I want to go home!'

'Well, you can't,' I said. 'We're on a mission.'

'I don't want to be on a mission! I didn't ask to come on a mission. I didn't volunteer!' Her voice rose to a shriek. Even the Queen tipped her head to one side; wondering, no doubt, how bats had got into the palace. The corgis, in a frenzy of excitement, rushed about the room, barking.

'I thought I told you to shut up!' the Queen yelled again, snatching her packet of biscuits and hurling it at them.

For a few seconds, the corgis were quiet, tearing and ripping to get at the biscuits.

'Funny,' I said to Rosie, 'how someone that's looked death in the face freaks out at the first sign of danger.'

Rosie's kneecaps were bouncing. 'Death didn't have a mouthful of teeth,' she said.

'Just put your jet pack on hover,' I said, 'and make sure you stay out of reach.'

'How do I p–p–put it on h–h–hover?'

I *knew* she hadn't taken it in! I reached across

and did it for her. I was beginning to realise that the success of our mission depended on me. Rosie might have looked death in the face, but you can't rely on someone who jeers at *Star Trek* and thinks it's all made up. Face them with a genuine emergency and they just go to pieces.

'What we have to decide,' I said, 'is who does what.'

Rosie looked at me, hopefully. 'Did this ever happen in *Star Trek*?'

I thought back. 'Something similar.'

'So you know all about it!' She sounded relieved. 'You know what to do.'

Sternly, I said, 'We both know what to do. The captain gave us our instructions. One of us gets the bug out, the other one zaps it.'

'All right,' said Rosie. 'I'll be the one that zaps it. You go and get it out.'

I hesitated.

'Well, go on, then!' She gave me a little shove. 'Sooner you do it, sooner we can get back.'

I gazed down, into the depths of the ravine. The corgis were still mopping up biscuit crumbs. The Queen was slurping her coffee, elbows on the table, mug clenched in both hands. I guessed it was the way she liked to do it, when she was alone. In public she would be far more refined.

As I watched, she put down the mug, settled some glasses on her nose, propped a magazine against the coffee pot and started to read. As she read, she picked biscuit crumbs out of her teeth. I thought it must be quite a relief for her, being able to do that. If she were at some banquet or something, she'd just have to keep sucking with her tongue and hoping nobody noticed. I began to feel a bit uncomfortable, watching the Queen pick her teeth. With her glasses and her crown, she looked just like the real Queen. Of course, she *was* the real Queen. Real Queen with an alien bug. I reminded myself that the bug had to be got out. *The bug had got to go.* Except...

How did we know there really was a bug? We'd been shown pictures of them, we knew what they looked like; but how did we know that one had actually got into the Queen? We didn't! All we had was the captain's word.

Suppose Rosie was right? Suppose he wasn't really the captain of a spaceship but a government agent? A *foreign* government agent. It could be a secret plot to kill the Queen!

'Are you going to do this, or not?' demanded Rosie.

I turned to face her, wobbled, and toppled over the edge. Quickly, I activated my jet pack and buzzed back up. By now the corgis had finished eating and were sniffing the air and pricking their ears. They had got wind of us! I tore open my bubble pack and threw down the contents, scattering them as best I could across the room.

'Well?' said Rosie.

'Thing is –' I hesitated.

'*What?*'

'How do we know she's got a bug? How do we know it's not just a plot?'

'Plot for what?'

'Plot to kill the Queen!'

'Oh. You mean, like … they're using us as hit men?' Rosie gave a triumphant snort. 'I told you they were government agents! It's obviously some kind of conspiracy.'

'What, our own government?'

'Yup.' She nodded. 'Our own government.'

I didn't understand. Why would our own government want to send hit men to get the Queen?

Rosie looked at me, pityingly. 'It's what governments do.'

'But why?' What had the Queen ever done to them?

'Who knows?' said Rosie. 'Only they have the answer to that.'

I frowned. This conversation didn't seem to be getting us anywhere – and the corgis were wolfing down dog biscuits as fast as they could go.

'I always knew there weren't such things as aliens,' said Rosie. 'I always said it was all in your imagination. Let's just tell them we've done what they wanted and get out.'

'But then they'll discover we haven't, and they'll just beam us back up again and –' I couldn't finish the sentence. I had these visions of being atomised and flung out, in a million pieces, into space.

'So what's your solution?' said Rosie.

I hung my head. I didn't have one.

'You know what?' Her voice rose to a shriek. 'This is a totally impossible situation and you're the one that went and got us into it, watching that stupid sci-fi stuff!'

'I beg your pardon,' I said, '*I* wasn't the one

84

that drew attention to myself, climbing out the bedroom window.'

'They would never have taken *me*,' said Rosie, 'if it hadn't been for *you*. So just go and do the job and let's get out!'

The corgis were gathering again, making little growls and snaps and jumping up at the wall.

'You're asking me to zap the Queen,' I said, horrified.

'Just a flesh wound,' said Rosie. 'That's all it needs. Then we can tell them we tried and it didn't work.'

'You do it,' I said.

'No way! It's your job.'

We stood, glaring at each other.

'Go and see if she's got a hole in her neck,' said Rosie. 'If there's a hole, it'll mean there's a bug. Then you can zap her and it'll be OK.'

'But suppose there isn't?'

'Then you zap her anyway, like in the arm, or something. And then we get out!'

I turned, fearfully, to look at the corgis. Then I looked across at the Queen. She'd finished picking her teeth. She slurped some more coffee, and yelled again at the corgis to shut up.

I guessed she must spend a lot of her time yelling at the corgis. Maybe if I aimed at her *foot*... Being zapped in the foot wouldn't kill her. It still seemed a terrible thing to do. Headlines flashed before my eyes: **BOY BREAKS INTO PALACE**. **INTRUDER SHOOTS QUEEN IN THE FOOT**. I couldn't do it!

And then the Queen stood up; and as I watched, goggle-eyed, she reached behind her with one hand and began vigorously scratching at her bottom. A sudden wave of relief rushed over me. It was true! *The Queen did have a bug.* She might pick her teeth in the privacy of her own palace; she might slurp her coffee and dunk her biscuits and yell at the corgis. But the Queen would *never* scratch her bottom. It was clear, at last, what I had to do.

'Right.' I nodded at Rosie. 'Open your bubble pack and scatter the contents. I'm going down to root out the bug. Be ready to zap it the minute it appears. OK?'

'So you think there really is a bug?' said Rosie. 'You really th—'

'Just do what I tell you,' I snapped, 'and don't argue!'

Rosie blinked. 'Yes, *sir*,' she said.

I waited till the corgis were safely occupied, fighting over the contents of Rosie's bubble pack, then zoomed down till I was on a level with the Queen's neck. She'd stopped scratching her bottom and was on her way to the door. I had to root out that bug before it was too late!

I hovered, trying to keep myself steady while I carefully picked through the Queen's hair, in search of a hole. Yes, there it was! Just as the captain had shown us. I was about to take aim when the Queen put up a hand and irritably slapped at the back of her neck. She was almost at the door. Frantically, I stuck the needle gun directly into the hole and fired.

There was a bloodcurdling shriek. But it didn't come from the Queen, it came from the bug. A slippery, slimy, glistening thing like a giant centipede, which shot out of the Queen's neck and fell hissing and spitting to the floor.

'Get it!' I shrieked at Rosie.

But Rosie was having trouble with her jet pack. Instead of floating just above the ground, out of reach of the corgis, she was down on the carpet … with the bug, writhing and slithering, making straight for her. I whizzed myself round, resetting my needle gun as I did so, but before I could get in a shot, one of the corgis had darted forward and snatched the thing between its teeth. Rosie rocketed back into the air, and I heard a satisfying *crunch* as the bug was bitten in two and swallowed. Phew! I felt the sweat dripping off me. That had been a bit too close for comfort.

I looked round for the Queen, to check she was all right. She had reached the door and was standing there, regally, waiting for the corgis.

'One has the strangest feeling,' she told them, 'that One has not been quite Oneself of late. But all of a sudden…' She smiled majestically. 'One feels quite restored. One is once again

Oneself!'

'Looks like we did it,' I said.

'Yeah, yeah, yeah, but now can we just get out?' begged Rosie. 'I've had enough of this!'

For once, I was in complete agreement. I pressed the button on my com badge and called through to the ship.

'Mission completed. Two to beam up!'

Chapter Ten

'Well done, Ensigns!' The captain was there to greet us as we beamed back aboard the ship. 'I knew we could rely on you!'

He held out a hand. With cheeks the colour of beetroot, I solemnly put mine into it. I could hardly believe it … Jake McGraw, shaking hands with the captain of the *Galactic Empire*!

'You have performed a great service, both to your country and to the universe.'

He turned to Rosie; but instead of taking his hand, Rosie very slightly shook her head and backed away. *Now* what was she up to?

'I didn't do anything,' she said.

'You were there,' said the captain.

'But I didn't *do* anything. It was all down to Jake. If it hadn't been for him, we'd never have got the job done. I just, like, totally *freaked*. He was the one got the bug out. He's the real hero.'

Wow! It was the nicest thing she'd ever said. Unfortunately, it made my cheeks practically burst into flames.

'Now I've embarrassed him,' said Rosie. 'But it happens to be true!'

'Well, that is honestly spoken,' said the captain. 'That is praiseworthy in itself.'

'Yeah. Thanks,' I muttered.

'Don't mention it.' Rosie waved a hand. 'I'd just really like to be getting home, now, if you don't mind.'

'Of course! I believe your mother wanted you back for lunch? Or, if you prefer, we could take you back earlier, to just before you were beamed up.'

'Lunch'd probably be best,' said Rosie. 'I wouldn't want to get into some kind of mad time loop and have to set off all over again. It was quite fun *once*,' she said, 'but I'd rather not make a habit of it.'

'How about you, Acting Ensign McGraw?' The captain turned, gravely, to look at me. 'May we call on you for another mission?'

I said, 'Yes, sir! Please, sir! Any time.'

'Well, that is good to know,' said the captain. 'As soon as we can arrange a new partner for you … I do have someone in mind. There is a girl called Lisa Lippincott –'

'Lisa Lippincott?' Rosie's head jerked up. 'She's in my class!'

'Yes; that is how we picked up on her.'

'Dunno what use she'd be.'

I couldn't very well say 'More use than you'. Not after she'd told the captain I was a hero.

'Of course, she is quite into science,' admitted Rosie. 'I suppose that'd help.'

'Rosie's more the literary type,' I said.

She flashed me a grateful smile. But it was the least I could do.

'Well, Acting Ensign…' The captain held out a hand. 'Here's to your next mission! And all future missions. We shall be in touch very soon.'

'Yes, sir! Thank you, sir!' I said.

'Lieutenant Malandra, could you do the honours?'

Lieutenant Malandra beamed us back down just as Auntie Jay and Uncle Kev were getting out of their car.

Auntie Jay said, 'Hello, you two! And what have you been up to?'

'Nothing very much,' said Rosie. 'Just back from the palace ... been rescuing the Queen from an alien bug.'

'Really?' Auntie Jay widened her eyes and gave a little shiver, making like she was impressed. 'That sounds pretty hairy!'

'Pretty hairy,' agreed Rosie.

'How did you rescue her?'

'Jake did it. He needle-gunned her and the bug shot out and one of the corgis ate it.'

'As corgis do,' said Uncle Kev, winking at Auntie Jay over our heads.

Mum had opened the front door and was waiting for us as we walked up the path.

'Guess what?' trilled Auntie Jay. 'Jake and Rosie have been rescuing the Queen from an alien bug!'

'Yes, they've been very busy that way just lately,' said Mum. 'Only yesterday they were abducted by aliens.'

'Well! Who says children don't use their imagination any more? You know what?' said Auntie Jay. 'You should write it all down!'

So that's what I've done. Not that I expect anybody to believe me...

James and the Alien Experiment

Sally Prue

*"The bony hand zoomed right out of
the screen and grabbed him."*

When James is kidnapped by aliens,
he can't believe his luck. They want to
transform his feeble human body and
James can have whatever superpowers he
likes. He chooses super-speed, super-brains
and super-strength. But James soon starts
to realise he might have got slightly
more than he asked for...

Black Cats
Books to pounce on

Time
AND AGAIN
Rob Childs

*"By a click of the clock, You can go in reverse,
Time and Again, For better or worse."*

With the discovery of a strange-looking
watch, twins Becky and Chris gain the
power to travel back in time. It's the
opportunity to relive events and put things
right. But trying to change the past doesn't
always work out as the twins intend.
Especially when class troublemaker
Luke is around…

Black Cats
Books to pounce on